Bride of
HA-HA! HORROR

MONSTERMATT PATTERSON

Mystery and Horror, LLC
Tarpon Springs, FL

Bride of
HA-HA! HORROR

Mystery and Horror, LLC
Tarpon Springs, FL
Copyright © 2015 by Mystery and Horror, LLC
First Trade Paperback Edition

Monstermatt Patterson, Author
Sarah E Glenn, Editor
Cover by: Monstermatt Patterson
Format and Layout by: Gwen Mayo
Introduction by: Monstermatt Patterson
Forward by: Zac Amico
Afterward by: Justin Martell

ISBN-13: 978-0996420945
(Mystery and Horror, LLC)

Printed in USA by Mystery and Horror, LLC
(www.mysteryandhorrorllc.com)

Book Praise and Prejudice

"Watch out for The Creature, and Monstermatt's terrible jokes!"

Julie Adams
Creature from the Black Lagoon

"Monster Matt's jokes want me to head back under the stairs and not only cut out my tongue, but take my eyes out!"

Sean Whalen
People Under the Stairs

"Monstermatt, for the love of all that is good in this world, stop - please stop - telling your awful jokes!"

John Amplas-Martin
Creepshow

"As a loyal friend of Monstermatt, I am offering free embalmings to those who die of laughter while reading this book."

Melantha Blackthorne
Death Race 2000

"Having co-produced and co-starred with Vincent Price in 130 hour-long episodes of the iconic pseudo horror kid's TV show The Hilarious House of Frightenstein, I know horror when I see it. Monstermatt Patterson's new volume two of HA-HA! HORROR's got it all, running the gamut from ghoulish to ghastly. His off-the-wall humor is scary, spooky, dark and verrry funny all wrapped up in one mummy-like reading experience, leaving no gravestones standing. No doubt about it, this series of books will become part of horror history!"

Mitch Markowitz
Hilarious House of Frightenstein

Dedication

In Loving Memory of my mother
Jean and my grandmother Mary.

Table of Contents

Introduction

Ghoul Mourning, Maniacs!!!

Yeshhhhhhhhhh!! That's right. It is I, your fiend, "Yours Drool-ly," Monstermatt Patterson! The Man of a Thousand Bad Monster Jokes, hailing all the way from Mattsylvania !!

Mwhuhuhahaha!!!

Today, I'm giving away The Bride of Ha-Ha! Horror. Not literally, Maniacs. You still have to pay retail. Igor! How does that saying about weddings go?

"You mean, the one about not dancing with your Monster-in-law?"

No, the other one! But, that is a good rule to live by. Have you ever seen her do "The ELECTRIC CHAIR Slide?". Yuck!

"Hey Master! Are you crying?"

No! It's allergies. I'm allergic to weddings! Let me see here...

Dearly Be-LOATHE-d,

We are CAPTURED here to ENDURE , I mean witness, the holy matri-MOANY of the Bride of Ha-Ha! Horror and my legion of Maniacs. Furthermore...ah, forget it.

"Master! Does 'legion' mean more than ONE Maniac?"

Quiet, Igor! Why don't you go soak your pointy little head? Aha! I have it! And before you utter a peep, Igor, I don't mean that I have poison oak or anything. Listen to this. You too, Maniacs.

Something BURROWED- that's you Igor, because you get under my skin!

Something GRUE- that'd be that old Monster-in-law!

A copy of The Sixth Sense in your shoe- or something like that.

Whatever, close enough! Here we go...

Maniacs, this time around there is a bucket full of jokes to give you all headaches and make you laugh!

Putrid Puns?

We got 'em! Rancid Rhymes?

You betcha! All that and more.

There's my 1400th, 1500th, 1600th and 1700th Bad Monster Jokes lurking about, waiting for you! And OF CORPSE, there are enough Horror biz types to roast me and poke fun of my jokes.

Note to self: I gotta start hanging with a better class of people! Sheesh!

So, get your shovel and dig right in to the fun! Call before you dig, because it's going to be a Gas!! See what I did there?

Mwhuhuhahaha!!

Acknowledgements

Monstermatt would like to thank the following people:

Mrs. Monstermatt and the Little Monsters. Deanna, Sarah, Grant, Emma. My loves.

Family. They're Kreepy and they're Kooky?

Naw, they're good.

The previous Roasters, and boy is this group expanding!

Joe Moe, Rodrigo Gudino, Joe Bob Briggs, Marcy Italiano, LL Soares, Greg Lamberson, Tony Moran, Nick Cato, Cornelius Badmonk, Pat Tantalo.

April Burril, Colleen Wanglund, Chris Alexander, Maria Olsen, Bill Oberst Jr., Tomb Dragomir, John Alan Schwartz, Tony Fayville, Kane Hodder, Michael Aliosi, Dr. Gangrene, Strange Jason and Michael Bonedigger.

The new roaster recruits:

Julie Adams, Zac Amico, Justin A. Martell, Melantha Blackthorne, Mitch Markowitz, Charles Band, John Amplas, Sean Whalen, Chris Olen Ray, Nathan Head, John Migliore, Greg Petaludis, Ron MacKay, Ari Lehman, Sephera Giron. These are some great ghouls!

Friends and institutions that keep this monster going:

J Ackermann and Famous Monsters of Filmland, Brian Wade, Rick Baker, Tom Savini, Sybil Danning, Debbie Rochon, The Gigante Family, Frank Henenlotter, The Horror Writer's Association, Amy Grech, Fangoria, Rue Morgue, Space Monsters Magazine, Zacherley, Svengoolie.

Elvira and all horror hosts

TROMA and all of its Lloyd Kaufman-led mutated inhabitants

Barbie Wilde and her Cenobite brethren- for humoring me while I humored them

The entire Western New York film, arts and haunted house communities

Brian Heiler, Sam Noir, Mego Museum, Plaid Stallions, The Lair of the Yak, Two Jews on Film, TOMB TV!!

Nora Drogi, Patrick Mallette, Sheri Litz, Arcana Studios.

We Love Monsters Magazine

Clifton Hill and especially the House of Frankenstein Wax Museum

The Hilarious House of Frightenstein

Christopher Lee, Vincent Price, Peter Cushing, Boris Karloff, Bela Lugosi, Ray Harryhausen

Benny Hill, Tex Avery

Mad Magazine

The North Tonawanda Public Library.

The FANGtastic fiends at Cats Like Us- Julie, Megan, Andrew. They are cool ghouls!!

A special thank you, to my childhood heroes, Adam West (Batman) and (Robin) Burt Ward.

My daughter and I met them at a huge convention in 2014, and I gave them copies of my previous book, "Ha-Ha! Horror".

Mr. West stood up and read my jokes to the crowd and he cemented his way further into my heart!

A special thank you, to Ms. Julie Adams and the Creature from the Black Lagoon, the inspiration for the cover's bride and groom. Julie was the first one to step up and roast me. A terrific person!!

Thank you, to the websites and shows I write for:

Horror Society.com, Horror News.Net, KillerAphrodite.com, The Retroist.com, TwistedCentral.com, GravediggersLocal.com, TombTV, 6FtPlus, Screamwave.

Thank you, Mystery & Horror LLC, Sarah Glenn and Gwen Mayo. Without your support, effort and belief, this project wouldn't be.

Finally, thank you to all of my Maniacs, readers and fans!! I enjoy writing and telling you jokes! It means the world to me. Whether we rub elbows at the various conventions, book signings or live shows, your reactions are what keep me wanting to create more gags. My, aren't you the YUCKY ones?! You've made "Bride of Ha-Ha! Horror" the new BLECHHH!

I suppose I should thank Igor and that weird, creepy thing sitting in the corner of the tomb. They're probably expecting it. Oh, baby!

Wait a minute... why does that ring a bell? Expecting ... Baby... Ohhhhhhhh Igor!!!

I'm having a bran storm, I mean, a brainstorm! I think we're expecting a "SON of" sometime in the future.

Oh, put the coffee on. Light the lights! Adore the doors! Ban the bannister! Oh, you know what I mean! It's time to write some Bad Monster Jokes!

Mwhuhuhahaha!!!!!

#OuijaBoardWishesCadaverDreams!

The Foreword

They say if you give one thousand monkeys one thousand type writers that they'll eventually come up with Shakespeare. Well, if all those monkeys had Ebola and were terrible joke writers, they'd write The Bride of Ha-Ha Horror.

The only thing horrific here is that "Monster" Matt Patterson is referred to as an author. Matt is an author in the same way that Jeffrey Dahmer was a celebrity chef. The only difference is Matt wouldn't last as long in prison.

I'd advise you to burn this book, but I wouldn't want that much unfunny to be released into the atmosphere all at once.

The transcript of the Nuremberg Trials has more laughs per page than this reprehensible read. "Monster" Matt Patterson is to comedy writing what Ed Gein is to furniture making.

In conclusion, Mr. Patterson has definitely written the perfect bathroom reader, and if you tear the pages in half you can get two wipes out of each one. The next time I see Matt's name in print, I sincerely hope it's in the Obituary Section.

In all seriousness,
Zac Amico
Troma

WHAT DID THE BRIDE GET FOR
FRANKENSTEIN'S MONSTER?

ENGRAVED NECKBOLTS!

WHAT WAS THE INSCRIPTION?

ONE NECKBOLT SAID "POSITIVE."
THE OTHER NECKBOLT SAID "NEGATIVE."

HA! WHAT A GREAT LITTLE JOKE ARC.
I HOPE YOU GOT AMPED UP OVER IT!

Universal Monsters Jokes

Where did Dracula buy a castle?
"VEIN-GORE, MAIM!"

Where was the Wolfman born?
"PAWtucket," Rhode Island!

The Invisible Man and Dracula opened a casting agency. They refused a play called "Reflections".
Why? Because they don't cast reflections!

Why was the Invisible Man mistaken for a Scientologist?
He went CLEAR!

What's the Wolfman's favorite FANGri-las song?

"LITTER of the Pack!"

Why can't Frankenstein's Monster use the "10 items or less" aisle?
His body has way more than 10 separate items!

What do you get by crossing Dracula and 'Lil Wayne?
Someone to suck your "BLOODIZZLERYP!"

Hear about the edgy comedy with the Wolfman and his pal?
It's called "HAIR-old & GHOUL-mar!"

Why did the Wolfman and Christine Aguilera have a karaoke battle?
To see who growled more!

What employment agency was started by the Mummy?
The "Im Ho TEMP" agency!

What kind of dirt lines Dracula's coffin?
Copies of the *Transylvanian Enquirer*!

What Lou Reed music transmits through Frankenstein's neck bolts?
The "VelVOLT" Underground!

Which Vampire is pretentious, but in a genteel way?
"DraculaLaDiDa!"

What's Quasimodo's favorite animal?
A BELL-uga Whale!

What do you get by crossing a *Miami Vice* wannabe film with the Mummy's Hand?
"The Mummy's Band of the Hand!"

What round of *Jeopardy* makes Frankenstein's Monster feel alive?
The LIGHTNING Round!

What kind of guitar does Dracula like?

The kind with a Double NECK!

Oh, I STRING you along!

Don't FRET. It's all a-CHORDING to plan!

What does Frankenstein's Monster think
of the Amazon FIRE phone?
FIRE, bad!!

Oh, the Monstrous world of finance has a
certain GRUE-p in hot water...

The Mummy is in it, deep. It seems he's
been selling PYRAMID schemes!

The Creature from the Black Lagoon is
just as fishy.
He's into POND-si schemes!

Frankenstein's Monster has STITCHED
together a scheme. Just like him, its
origins are from parts unknown.

Dracula has been draining bank
accounts. Blood and otherwise.

The Wolfman's dealings have gotten a
little HAIRY.
He's accused of the old "BITE and
Switch!"

—
6

Dr. Jekyll is a rough salesman. He's been gouging prices AND eyes!

Quasimodo went to the NYSE. He just wanted to ring the opening bell!

It's been said that Dr. Frankenstein used Wonder Bread to make his Monster, because it "builds better bodies." That's not true. Everyone knows it has more chemicals than Lindsey Lohan!

What did The Bride get for Frankenstein's Monster?
Engraved Neckbolts!

What was the inscription?
One neckbolt said "positive."
The other neckbolt said "negative."

Ha! What a great little joke ARC.
I hope you got AMPED up over it!

Who is Lawrence Talbot's favorite Quebec Nordique?
"WOLF Paiment!"

Who is Lawrence Talbot's favorite St. Louis Blue?
Bernie "FUR-derko!"

What beer does Dracula like?
"Dos NECKIES!"

Stay Blood thirsty, my friends!

Bad news: Im Ho Tep got a concussion. No word on whether he'll suffer any "MUMMY-ry loss." Good news: His head was already bandaged.

Why doesn't Dracula want to be on trial? He'll crumble under CROSS examination!

Which Vampire bit and made Jamie Foxx and T-Pain famous?

Blame it on Dra-a-a-a-a-acula!

Blame it on Dra-a-a-a-a-acula!

Oh, Dracula digs music.

He thinks "Waiting for the Sun" by The Doors describes his nightly activities.

What lyric from *Annie* does Dracula hate?
"The Sun will come out, tomorrow!"

What *Fiddler on the Roof* song does Dracula have a love/hate relationship with?
"Sunrise, Sunset!"

What Beatles song can Dracula do without?
"Good Day, Sunshine!"

What is Van Helsing's favorite Sammy Hagar song?
"I Can't Drive 55... Stakes into Dracula!"

What film has Shirley McClain and Clint Eastwood tracking an underground group?
"Two Mole People for Sister Sarah!"

There's been some chit chat around the blood cooler. Here's what we overheard...

"I must be really shallow. People see right through me!"
- The Invisible Man

"Yes, I'll be an organ donor. You can have my Wurlitzer when I retire."
- The Phantom of the Opera

"We can have a successful underground movement."
- The Mole People

"It's 'We belong dead,' this, 'We belong dead,' that. Can't we go on with our afterlife, already?"
- The Bride of Frankenstein

"The children of the night, what music they make... and it's WAYYY past the local noise ordinances!

Give a Vampire a break!!"
- Dracula

WHAT DOES THE CREATURE FROM THE BLACK LAGOON "USE A LITTLE DAB OF" TO KEEP HIS POMPADOUR NEAT?

KRILL CREME!

Creature from the Black Lagoon Jokes

Whatever the Creature from the Black Lagoon does, he wants to make a big splash.

I met the Creature's friend. His name is Phil. Phil "Leighophish!"

The Creature is so famous...
He's so famous, that he's getting a STARFISH on the Hollywood SWIM of Fame!

How does the Creature from the Black Lagoon say "Farewell" in Italian?
"A-REEF-ederci!"

What famous explorer does the Creature from the Black Lagoon admire?

SEABASStion Cabot!

What TV show scares the Creature from the Black Lagoon?
Drag-NET!

What *Gilligan's Island* actress does the Creature from the Black Lagoon love?
TUNA Louise!

What Mark Twain story does the Creature like?
The Adventures of Huckleberry FINS!

What's the Creature's favorite Monty Python film?
Life of BRINE!

When it comes to swimming, the Creature from the Black Lagoon is an "A-Fishy-anado."

What fraternity does the Creature from the Black Lagoon belong to?
CLAMbda CLAMbda CLAMbda!

Who is the Creature's favorite performer?
Kylie MINNOWgue!

I thought the Creature from the Black Lagoon wasn't paying attention to what I was saying. It turns out that he needed batteries for his HERRING aid!

Who is the Creature from the Black Lagoon's favorite Star Trek character?
Captain PIKE!

And last, but not least- the 1500th Bad Monster Joke, featuring old Gilman himself...

What does the Creature from the Black Lagoon "use a little dab of" to keep his pompadour neat?
KRILL-Creem!

WHY DID JASON BUY A MONKEY WITH A TIN CUP?

TO OPERATE A "HURT-Y GURDY!"

Friday the 13th Jokes

Did you know Jason was an actor?
He auditioned for a part in "HACK to the Future!"

What's Jason's favorite Simon & Garfunkel song?
"50 Ways to Kill Camp Counselors!"

Who do you get by crossing a Jason Vorhees actor with Kathy Lee's co-star?
KANE Hoda!

What show does Jason watch Mrs. Scare-ette on?
The HACKS of Life!

What fraternity does Jason belong to?
"Phi -DECAPITATE -A!"

At the end of the first *Friday the 13th*, Jason (played by Ari Lehman) pops up from the lake, attacking a boat. His understudy noted the boat to be "quick and easily maneuvered." His name was YAR-i Lehman.

Jason has come back more times than that awful fruitcake you keep regifting at Christmas!

What quiz show do Jason Vorhees and Michael Myers want to compete on? "SLASH Cab!"

Why did Jason buy a monkey with a tin cup? To operate a "HURT-y Gurdy!"

Jason follows the "what doesn't kill you makes you stronger" train of thought, quite literally. I literally wish he would take a train right out of town!

What do you get by crossing Jason Vorhees, Freddy Krueger and a Hobbit? FRODO vs. Jason!

What's Jason's favorite arts and crafts activity?
"MacraMAIM!"

BATMAN & ROBIN THE BUOY WONDER!

WHAT DO YOU GET WHEN YOU CROSS VIN-
CENT PRICE AND ALFRED E. NEUMANN?

MADHOUSE!

Miscellaneous - General

Hear about the artist who sculpts with heating & cooling systems?
His work is rather "Air Vent Garde!"

He BREEZED through his first piece.

He was inspired by his wife, WINDY.

He was also inspired by their daughter Eva Porator, and his mother, FLOW.

What Spike Lee joint features the Flintstones?
"YabbaDabbaDoo the Right Thing!"

Who created a communist movement at a sub shop?
HOAGIE Min!

He also created an eight foot communist party sub!

I just heard that a TV show about tornadoes is getting a "spin off" program.

Would Morgan FREEMAN be cast in the PRISONER?

What MC Young song do sculptors like? "BUST a Move!"

I was told to join a twelve step program for my cookie habit. Thankfully, it was only twelve steps. Any more, and I'd be winded.

"Whaaaat" does rapper 'Lil John celebrate on December 31st? "New YEEEAHHH'S Eve!"

If a tree falls in the forest, does anybody hear? No one cares anymore, but if a tree falls and hits you in the crotch, it winds up on *Tosh*!

Did you hear about the Jane Austen martial arts film?
It's called "Sensei and Sensibility!"

Hear about the demolitions expert who moonlighted as a hip hop artist?
Man, he could "Break it down!"
They say web designers go to bed "URL-ly."

What do you get by crossing an actor from *The Producers* and an 80's drug addiction film?
"Less Than Zero Mostel!"

The song, "On a Slow Boat to China" has been updated to: "On a Slow, Lead-Poisoned Boat From China."

He told her, "Shake your money maker!"
But, she couldn't lift her scanner and printer at the same time.

Hear about the Smurf comedian?
He only worked "BLUE!"

Why do witches watch the first two
Home Alone movies?
To see Macaulay "CAULDRON!"

I tried watching a TAPE about
ADHESIVES, but I couldn't STICK with it.
It moved at a snail's PASTE. Yet,
somehow it got GLUING reviews.

What group of juggaloes does "cloud
computing?"
The Insane CLOUD Posse!

Then there was the chef who cooked
everything with intense bursts of heat.
He was so SEAR-ious about his cooking
style.

What actor do you get by crossing Eddie
Murphy's version of Buckwheat and the
actor who played Mel Sharples?
Vic "OTAY-back!"

I only want to hear the phrase "Honey
Boo-Boo" if Yogi Bear says, "Hey, look at
this picnic basket! It's full of honey, Boo-
Boo!"

Then, there was the guy who thought The Weather Channel was getting racy. He heard they had a special about "weather STRIPPING."

What superhero fights against the words that accompany photos?
"CAPTION America!"

What do you get by crossing a Johnny Depp film and a Hanna-Barbera cartoon about a purple giant?
"What's Eating Gilbert Grape Ape?"

How does Spiderman self-diagnose?
WEB MD!

Why did Spiderman appear on *Tosh.0*?
For a WEB redemption!

A fella watched *HOPE Floats* starring Sandra Bullock.
Then, he watched a LESLIE Nielsen film.
Then, he listened to DEVO and TED Nugent.

He sang "Happy Birthday, TO YOU!" to his friend.
After all of this, what "Grease" song did he have stuck in his head?

"HOPE floats, LES-LIE Nielsen, DEVO-TED Nugent, happy birthday TO YOU!" (GROAN is the word)

What is George Hamilton's favorite gem? "TAN-zanite!"

A bat was using sonar to guide its flight. The bat was almost home, but it was experiencing difficulties. It seemed SONAR, yet, so far away.

What seafood reminds you of *Lassie* and Connie Chung's husband?
"COLLIE MAURY!"

George Hamilton is a respected SPFX artist. That's "Sun Protection Factor Effects."

Then, there was the guy who thought *The Maltese Falcon* was a bird who enjoyed taunting people in food courts.

What music does the Human Torch like? Waka Flaka "FLAME On!"

WHAT IS TOM CULLEN'S FAVORITE BOOK?

GOODNIGHT M-O-O-N!

Rosemary's Baby Jokes

Hear about Rosemary's favorite devilish British cop?
He's "Rosemary's BOBBY!"

What public affairs network does Rosemary's Baby watch?
"C-SPAWN!"

What film is about the spawn of a favorite singer?
"Rosemary Clooney's Baby!"

What film is about a woman involved with a fancy sound system?
BOSEmary's Baby!"

What film deals with a couple that is split 50/50 about having kids?

"Rosemary's MAYBE!"

Hear about Rosemary's Baby?
He had a "Devil May Care" attitude!

What film is about the spawn of an
olfactory specialist?
"NOSEmary's Baby!"

Which baby is the spawn of a sheer
tights salesman?
"HOSEmary's Baby!"

What happened when Shrek's friend
Donkey, saw Rosemary's Baby?
He BRAYED for them!

What slug line was written by a sculptor?
CLAY for Rosemary's Baby!

They say Rosemary's Baby was very
"SPAWNtaneous!"

What was Rosemary's Baby's birthstone?
Brimstone!!

WHEN A "WRECKING BALL" MEETS A REAL BALL
THAT REALLY CAUSES DAMAGE...

Cat People Jokes

Why is there a *Cat People* remake with Rev. Al Sharpton?
Well, according to him, "He's not a Rat, he's a Cat!"

With their Nine lives, it's doubtful the Cat People subscribe to the idea of "YOLO" (You. Only. Live . Once.)

What new video format was *Cat People* rereleased in?
"Litter Boxed Edition!"

When they filmed *Cat People*, there were nondisclosure agreements filed on set, so nobody let the Cat People out of the bag!

Cat People was going to have a dance number. It was going to be led by "CHEETAH Rivera!"

Did you know the Cat People were politically active? They fought for their CIVET liberties!

Why do fans like *Cat People*?
It's a "PAWS-ible" story!

The Cat People believe in "CLAWS and effect!"

What do you get by crossing Mad Max and a Warriors rival gang?

"Mad Max: Furies Road!"

Mad Max: Fury Road Jokes

What film has Mad Max searching for McDonald's cold treats?
"Mad Max: MCFLURRY Road!"

Mad Max: Fury Road had more family squabbles than the Jacksons!

What happens when you cross an 80's computer-generated PPP icon with the Road Warrior?
You get Mad Max Head, Head, Headroom!

What film follows Mad Max on a quest to find people dressed like animals?
"Mad Max: Furries Road!"

What do you get by crossing Mad Max and a Warriors rival gang?

"Mad Max: Furies Road!"

What film stars Phil Silvers in a cross country treasure hunt?
It's a Mad, Mad, Mad, Mad, Mad Max: Fury Road World!"

Who was the *Mad Max: Fury Road* heroine with a "deviated septum?"
"Imperator FuriNOSEa!"

What did the War Boy say after hearing "Que Sera, Sera?"
"What a Day. What a lovely Doris Day!"

What film was about a quest for garbage bags?
"GLAD Max: Garbage Road!"

What Mad Max film had a quest for Dacron?
"Mad SLACKS: Polyester Road!"

Which Mad Max heroine was named after an Indian dish?
Imperator "FuriDOSA!"

What do you get by crossing a Mad Max film and cataracts?
"Mad Max: BLURRY Road!"

WHAT DO YOU GET BY CROSSING THE
BABADOOK WITH A STAR WARS BOUNTY
HUNTER?

THE "BOBADOOK!"

The Babadook

What do you get by crossing two cousins and a monster hiding under their "General Lee" car?
The "BabaDUKES of Hazzard!"

What film has a haunted thief and his wife who unleashes a popup book's monster every night?
"The BABADOOK , The Thief, His Wife and Her Lover!"

The Platters are joining in on the popup book monster craze, with their song "The BABADOOK, DOOK, DOOK of Earl!"

What popup book monster comes out when someone says, "Open Sesame?"
"Ali BABADOOK!"

Head about the popup book monster
who droned on and on?
They call him- "BLAH, BLAH,
BLAHbadook!"

What popup book monster floats on
water?
"The BOBadook!"

What popup book monster haunts
Goodfellas?
The "MOBadook!"

Hear about the Babadook's kleptomaniac
cousin?
He's the "BabaTOOK!"

What monster pops out of Aflac
pamphlets?
The "BabaDUCK!"

What do you get by crossing the
Babadook with a Star Wars bounty
hunter?
The "BOBAdook!"

What monster pops up and haunts Marty McFly?
The "BabaDOC!"

What do you get by crossing the Babadook and a nursery rhyme?
"Babadook Sheep!"

WHAT DO YOU GET BY COMBINING PINOCCHIO
AND DRACULA?

NOSEFERATU!

The Crawling Hand Jokes

What airline does the Crawling Hand use?
"LuftHANDSA!"

When the Crawling Hand heard that "hands free" was popular, he thought he'd never spend another dime!

Does the Crawling Hand ever feel "Knuckleheaded?"

Which "Golden Girl" does the Crawling Hand like?
"Rue MclanaHAND!"

What exercises keep the Crawling Hand "rough and tough?"
"CALLUSED-thenics!"

Which movie monster was a stunt double in "The Slap?"
The Crawling Hand!

Which actor does the Crawling Hand admire?
"Sydney POINTER FINGER!"

WHAT DO VAMPIRES WEAR WHEN PRACTICING
THE DOWNWARD BAT?

COUNT YORGA PANTS!

The Swarm Jokes

What type of music did they listen to while filming *The Swarm*?
"BEE-BOP!"

Which *Golden Girls* actress should've started in *The Swarm*?
"Bee Arthur!"

Did you know there are two classes of bees?
"The HIVES and the HIVE nots!"

Which actor auditioned for *The Swarm*?
Jeffery "HONEYcombs!"

What did *The Swarm* crew like to eat while filming?
Bagels with sour cream and HIVES!

Who was the lead actor in *The Swarm*?
BUZZ!

Why was the bee actor hard to
understand?
He was a "MUMBLE Bee!"

What auction site was used on set?
BEEzid!

What kind of car was given to the cast
and crew?
Corvette "STINGray!"

Which comedienne was brought in to
provide laughs?
Ruth "BUZZ-y!"

Which member of The Police do the bees
like?
STING!

Who directed *The Swarm*?
"Paul-Inator!"

WHAT'S MEDUSA'S FAVORITE E. L.O. SONG?

TURN TO STONE!

Miscellaneous Horror

What murderous duo sold their victims to barbershops?
Burke & "HAIR!"

Judging by its configuration, I would guess the Human Centipede uses LinkedIn for its social network.

Hear about the Joan Crawford/Bette Davis reboot?
It's called "Whatever Happened to Baby Jane's Facebook Page?"

What about a Peter Lorre film reboot?
It's called "The Beast With Five MySpace Pages!"

Alfred is getting modern, with "The Angry BIRDS!"

What do you get by crossing a Ray Bradbury novel and an Internet encyclopedia page?

"Something WIKIPEDIA This Way Comes!"

The Spirit world was upset, because Facebook wanted to change the settings on all Ouija boards.

Some experts say the Necronomicon is the original "Face Book."

How do you know you're at a séance for a texting spirit?

The Ouija board spells out "O.M.G.!"

What film combines fake friend requests and a mysterious alien stowaway?
"It! The Terror Beyond MySpace!"

(I heard it influenced "Facehugger Book")

What Edgar Alan Poe story is about an Internet plague?
"Masque of the REDDIT Death!"

Why won't Dorian Gray join Facebook?
He's afraid someone will report his picture!

What game company do the Alligator People like?
"MOLTING Bradley!"

Duane and Belial, from *Basket Case*, enjoy games from "HASBRO connected to his side."

What company makes toys that a Cyclops loves?
"EYE-Deal!"

Hear about the messy morgue?
It was really unORGANized!

How does Michael Crichton drain his pasta?
With an "Andromeda Strainer!"

What film do you get by crossing *The Tool Box Murders* and a James Bond film?
"A View to a DRILL!"

Which Hammer Films actress loves old video games?
Ingrid "PITTfall!"

Which one of Ingrid Pitt's films starred Danny and Crispin?
"The Vampire GLOVERS!"

If they remade *The Incredible 2-Headed Transplant* with Jack Black and Jack White, would there be any GRAY areas?

What do you get by crossing Michael Myers and a trumpet player?
"Horn Stabs!"

What does Buffalo Bill say when he's at the beach?
"It puts the lotion on its skin, or it gets sunburned again."

What new film combo are they making with Peter Cushing and Edward Burns? "Seven Brides of Dracula for Seven Brothers McMullen!"

I just heard a terrific speech by Swamp Thing. He opened with "WEED my lips..."

If *The Karate Kid* were a monster movie, would there be a Mr. MiyOGRE?"

Ahhh...Wax on, Demon Son...

What kind of camera should Hannibal Lecter get to film himself with Agent Starling?
A "Quid GO-PRO" Camera!

Hear about the standup comedian cadaver?
His tag line is, "Well, EXHUUUMME, Me!"

What TV show do the Killer Shrews like?
"La-VERMIN & Shirley!"

I heard Dr. Caligari say, "There's nothing in these cabinet instructions about a Sleepwaker! I'll never shop IKEA again!"

How do you know the Terminator is happy?
He has SPRINGS in his steps! A few other parts too...

What cartoon features the hiking of Karen Black and a tiny, terrorizing doll?
"ZUNI Toons!"

Hear about the new bank on Dr. Moreau's island?
It's the H.G. WELLS Fargo Bank!

Sharon Stone and Michael Douglas are back at it. Their next project is about giant ants. It's called "Basic INSECT!"

The Frozen Dead is due for a remake.
It'll be produced by the Bird's Eye Company!
I heard the leading man is "REFRIGERATOR Perry."
The script has a "Best if used by" date.

Which "Charlie's Angel" did Damien
Thorne think was his real mother?
"JACKAL-Lynn Smith!"

In *The Exorcist* what evil was Father
Karras trying to get rid of?
The unwanted U2 album in Reagan's
Ipod!

Which TV host is known to Monsters?
"SCAR-son Daly!"

What's a pickup line between two
Triffids?
"Hey! Nice STEMS!"

What film combines car sharing and
Stephen King's story of a machine
takeover?
"Maximum ÜBER-drive!"

What happens when you cross a prom
revenge and Conan the Barbarian's god?
"CROM Night!"

Dione Warwick's cousin Dione GORE-wick, covered her song. It's called, "Do You Know the WRAITH in San Jose?"

What happened to the scifi fan on trial?

His lawyer told him to plead the "FIFTH Element!"
(Can I get a "multi pass" on this one?)

Robocop has been policing fraternities. He's now known as "WHOA, BROCOP!"

HBO is combining its shows. Get ready for
"TrueBlood Detectives!"

This reminds me of the Matthew McConaughey Vampire flick-
"The Dallas BITERS Club!"

What Edgar Alan Poe story is about "Foodies?"
"The Falafel of the House of Usher!"
Directed by Barbara "Ganoush!"

What did the Morlocks first think of the Eloi?
They were just beginning to scratch the surface... people.

What *Andy Griffith Show* character is beloved by Maniacs and Monsters?
"Gomer VILE!"

Hear about the wonderful German Werewolf?
He was "WunderBARK!"

What Mark Twain story does Michael Myers like?
"KNIFE on the Mississippi!"

Werewolves like Mark Twain's story "RiffRUFFing It!"

What do you get by crossing Rudy Ray Moore and underground mutants?
"The MOLEmite People!"

Why are the Triffids such good gymnasts?

Every time they land, they PLANT their feet!

How does Godzilla evade speed traps on Monster Island?
He uses his "RODAN detector!"

Where does Arnold Cunningham hope to donate Christine?
"1-877-Killer Kars for Kids!"

What story does Medusa read to the snakes on her head?
"Little Red WRITHING Hood!"

What's Medusa's favorite ELO song?
"Turn to STONE!"

What's a jazz love song for horror fans?
"Bueno SCARE-A, Bueno SCARE-A, SCREAM-orina..."

What do Vampires wear when practicing the "Downward BAT?"
"Count YORGA Pants!"

After a workout in those, you should GHOUL down.

What famous cabaret do the Mole People like?
The "MOLE-in Rouge!" It's got a real UNDERGROUND vibe!

What dish honors the *ABC's of Death*?
Alphabet Soup with Cyanide broth!

I heard the next *Sharknado* will be filmed in FISHKILL, NY!

What TV show does Stephen King's Firestarter watch?
"BURN Notice!"

What film combines Barbara Steel and Legos?
"BLOCK Sunday!"

How do Cannibals start arguments during lunch?
One of them says," Don't you give me any LIPS!"

Never lend books to CUJO. They always come back "DOG eared."

The Leprechaun is suing me. He's taking me to "Small MAIMS" Court!

What Thomas Harris themed restaurant serves a Tooth Fairy burger?
"Red Dragon! Yum!"

What Full Moon film is a biopic of Jared, from Subway?
"SUB Species!"

Do you know what vegetarian horror fans like?
"Arue-GHOUL-A!"

What film combines the Four Seasons and a Cryptid?
"The Jersey Devil Boys!"

What's a Monster's favorite condiment?
"MAIMonaise!"

What do Monsters put on their burgers?
"RHARRAGHlish!"

What Karen Carpenter song is inspired by Michael Crichton's work?
"Andromeda Strain-y Days and Mondays!"

What film is about a resort full of Ghosts?
"The Grand BOOOO-dapest Hotel!"

What film is about U2's guitarist?
"The EDGE of Tomorrow!"

What film is about FX artists and their latex injury makeups?
"The Vault of Our SCARS!"

How do adult Ghosts combat "ectoplasmic dysfunction?"
They take the "Little BOO Pill!"

What film has a woman trying to pawn an antique murderous mirror?
"HOCK-ulus!"

What film is about giant insects and an 80's band?

"Adam & THEM Ants!"

What ancient evil terrorizes Haddonfield every 52nd Halloween?
"Michael MAYANS!"

I'm certain that Zombies like the song "Back to Life" by Soul to Soul. It's their jam!

Which one of the Outsiders wrote *The Raven*?
"POEnyboy Curtis!"

What happens if you put Jon Cryer's *Pretty in Pink* character in a *Child's Play* film?
You get "The Bride of DUCKIE!"

What film has Peter Cushing and the "power to do more?"
"Frankenstein and the Monster from DELL!"

What three headed Kaiju loves to sing?
"GLEEdorah!"

What film is about a disfigured musician willing to sell his soul to stop gambling? "Phantom of the Pair of Dice!"

Hear about the new haunted bread?
It has "twelve whole GROANS!"

They say I'm a BRAT. It's true- I'm at my WURST. It's no BALONEY!

How do fights start on Monster Island?
Godzilla says "Yo MOTHRA sooo ugly!"

What Florence and the Machine song makes CUJO nervous?
"The DOG days are over!"

Which *Three's Company* character is a combo of Norman Fell and Death?
"The Grim ROPER!"

Which Black Eyed Pea is a fan of Richard Matheson?
"Will-I-Am Legend!"

What's a chip for cheap Zombies?
"FreeToes!"

PENELOPE PITSTOP AND THE PENDULUM!

THE FROG

Women in Horror Month

What do you get by crossing a Jessica Cameron film with a John Waters musical?
"Truth or Hairspray!"

What do you get by crossing a Jovanka Vuckovick film and a Goldie Hawn/Mel Gibson team up?
"Captured Bird on a Wire!"

Have you ever heard of Chainsaw Sally? She's got nerves of STIHL!

Danielle Harris. Oh, Danielle Harris. Please make more horror films and scare us!

Debbie Rochon's directorial debut mixes fantasy and a life or death contest. It's called "The Model Hunger Games!"

Melantha Blackthorne, dear friend of mine. Please take the six second challenge and put some videos on the Vine.

The Twisted Soska Twins have incredible matching grins. Rivaled by their incredible creations. Their zest for bloody film sets, is infectious in all horror nations.

To all the women we love, in horror. You've smashed down a lot of doors. I decapitate this tune, no doubt that you'll swoon - to all the women we love, in horror.

What actress do Androids like? Adrienne "Bar-BOLTED!"

Ugh! Now Igor wants to jump in. I wish he'd jump into an acid bath. Oh well. Go ahead, Igor.

"Thank you, Master."

Debbie Rochon came to town, to star in a horror movie. She sat with me for the lunch break and showed me her two..."

IGOR!!!! P-p-please tell me this doesn't end how I think it will? We've got a respectable bunch of Maniacs reading this! Or is it despicable? Umm... either way, I'm afraid to let you continue.

"Master, it's ok. Listen: She showed me her two SMOOTHIES!! "

Igor?! What are you talking about? Two smoothies? Who buys two?!

"She bought one and got one for free. She gave me one. End of story. What did you think I meant?!"

Umm... Never mind. Anyway...

What Screamqueen is keen on pronounciation ?

SYLLABLE Danning!!

What duo of *Laverne & Shirley* neighbors
involves a Screamqueen?
Linnea & Squiggy!!

SNACK PLISSKEN

American Horror Story Jokes

What antique hunting show goes through a haunted house, an insane asylum, a coven, and a Freakshow?
"American Horror Story Pickers!"

What song does Jimmy the Lobster boy hate?
"She's a BISQUE House!"

What can the twins in *AHS* Freakshow sing?
"I'm looking over, one of our shoulders!"

What *AHS* season spins a tale about a certain body of water?
"American Horror Story CREEK Show!"

What do they say about Pepper?
"She's the SALT of the earth!"

What TV show haunts smokers?
"American Horror STOGIE!"

What TV show haunts restless sleepers?
"American Horror SNORE-y!"

Hear about the *American Horror Story*
Coven softball team?
They were "WITCH hitters!"

How close were the networks of witches
in *American Horror Story*?
So close, they were like "Kissing
COVENS!"

What *AHS* actress used hip phrases in
her dialogue?
"Jessica SLANG!"

What do you get by crossing *AHS* with
Mel Brooks?
"American Horror Story of the World:
Part 1!"

What do you get by crossing an Eddie Griffin super spy and the third season of *AHS*?
"American Horror Story UnderCOVEN Brother!"

THE UNDERWATER NAZI ZOMBIES WERE "SS" SOLDIERS.

IT MEANS "SYNCHRONIZED SWIMMERS!"

Shock Waves Jokes

What do you get by crossing underwater Nazi zombies and a Vulcan?
"SPOCK Waves!"

What brand of tuna was spawned by "Shock Waves?"
"Underwater Nazi Zombies of the Sea!"

Who was the leading lady in *Shock Waves*?
"Flo-Tationdevice!"

Who was the underwater Nazi zombies' favorite cartoon dog?
"SCUBA-Doo!"

What hair care product sponsored *Shock Waves*?
AQUA Net!

The underwater Nazi zombies were a few islands down from Italy. They had underwater NUNZIO zombies!

What is the underwater Nazi zombies' favorite band?
"Katrina and the Shock Waves!"

The underwater Nazi zombies like singing along with the Soggy Bottom Boys. They really identify with them!

The underwater Nazi zombies were "SS" soldiers. It means "Synchronized Swimmers!"

The underwater Nazi zombies were a little naive. You could say they were "wet behind the ears." Well, there and everywhere else!

What did the *Shock Waves* zombies call their base of operations?
"H2QO!"

What did the underwater Nazi zombies call that wafting smell from their waterlogged footwear?
"SOCK Waves!"

LET'S TWISTY AGAIN, LIKE WE LAST SUMMER!

Wishmaster Jokes

What do you get by crossing a demonic Djinn and laundry soap?
"WASH-master!"

What's the Wishmaster's favorite drink?
A "Slow DJINN Fizz!"

What's the Wishmaster's favorite type of cookie?
What, were you expecting DJINN-gerbread? Man, you're worse than me! Sheesh!

Did you hear about the Djinn who had sudden fast movements?
They called him "WOOSH-master!"

Hear about the Djinn who was named "Timex"?

They called him "WATCHmaster!"

What do you get by crossing the Wishmaster and Jay Leno?
A CHIN!

What do you get by crossing a Djinn and a college radio band?
"Was Not WAS-master!"

Which Djinn would assemble his wishes?
"The Wish-MUSTER!"

Which Djinn wasn't very decisive?
"The WishWashyMaster!"

What did they call the Djinn with wet, muddy shoes?
The "SQUISH-master!"

Why did the Wishmaster go to the dentist?
He had "DJINNgivitis!"

Which Djinn grants people extra bottles of salad dressing?
"WISHBONE-master!"

"NEIL BEFORE ZOD..."

WHICH CENOBITE WANTS TO COMPETE
ON DANCING WITH THE STARS?

DR. CHA-CHA-CHANNARD!!

Hellraiser Jokes

In what film does Mel Gibson's ghost come back to evade the Cenobites?
"Mel Raiser!"

What do you get by crossing the stars of *Mad About You* with the Cenobites?
"Hell Reiser!"

In *Hellraiser: Hellbound* what torch song crooner turns into Pinhead?
"Mel Tore my soul apart!"

What puzzle box do you get by crossing *Hellraiser* and "Sanford & Son"?
"The LAMONT Configuration!"

Which Cenobite wants to compete on *Dancing With the Stars*?
"Dr. Cha-Cha-CHANNARD!"

What website is devoted to the Cenobites?
"Pinhead-terest!"

What do you get by crossing singing food with the Cenobites?
"HellRAISINS!"

What Swing era song is about a Cenobite?
"Pardon me Clive, is that the Chatterbox ChooChoo?!"

If the Cenobites played football with Uncle Frank and Julia, how they make teams?
"Shirts and NO SKINS!"

If the Cenobites come when you solve their puzzle, will they "tear souls apart?" Nope they're here to Nancy Grace a muzzle! That's definitely a start.

One of the Cenobites had numbness in his leg. He described it as having "Pinheads and needles!"

How do Butterball and friends achieve a "total state of focus?"
They're "ZENobites!"

"THEN, IT'S OFF TO THE COMIC STRIPS...
WITH THE SUCCESS OF "AFTERLIFE WITH
ARCHIE" WE WANT...

"BRINGING UP FATHER FROM HIS GRAVE."
MAGGIE HAS TO DEAL WITH JIGGS IN THIS
AFTERLIFE ADVENTURE!

HEAR ABOUT THE ALIEN CHESTBURSTER WHO
CAN ACT?

HE'S DUE FOR A BREAKOUT PERFORMANCE!

Monstermatt Minute Jokes

What do Dr. Frankenstein and Herbert West have in common?
They're both from "REGENERATION X!"

What is a grave digger's favorite nursery rhyme?
"Little Jack MOURNER!"

Hear about the *Alien* chest burster that acts?
He's due for a "breakout" performance!

Ever wonder if the Invisible Man's favorite Beatles song is, "I'm Looking Through You?"

They say Freddy Krueger clawed his way to the top... of many bodies.

Which Sousa march do the Terminators like?
"Old IRONsides!"

Which Sousa March does Frankenstein's Monster like?
"Ben NECK BOLT!"

What legal drama does MechaGodzilla like?
"ALLOY McBeal!"

Which actress wants to appear in a Ouija board film?
"Cate PLANCHETTE!"

What kind of scientist studies my crummy jokes?
A "STALE-ontologist!"

Don't ever threaten a cannibal with a "knuckle sandwich." They'll take that offer.

Who is Sweeney Todd's favorite NBA team?

———

The LA CLIPPERS!

What weight loss supplement does Sweeney Todd use?
TRIM Spa!

What Peter Gabriel song does Zira sing to Taylor in *Planet of the APES*?"
"In Your BRIGHT EYES!"

Who is older, Joan Collins or Barnabas Collins from *Dark Shadows*?
Doesn't matter, they're both "VAMPY!"

The cannibals are cooking out. I think they'll cool up some Franks... and some other guys.

Also on the menu:

Water Melanie chunks.
Diced Marisa Tomei-toes
A fashionable serving of Kenneth Cole-slaw
A serving of John McEnroe-knee and cheese.

What kind of pants does the average horror fan wear?
DunGORE-ees-!

What do you get by crossing an Edgar Alan Poe story with the *Wacky Races* cartoon?
"Penelope PITstop and the Pendulum!"

When I heard Clive Barker wrote *Thief of ALWAYS*, I thought-why would anyone steal a Richard Dreyfus movie?

Which original *SNL* actor is beloved by monsters?
GORE-ate Mortis!

I heard Hedwig (*Harry Potter*) the owl and Bubo (*Clash of the Titans*) are starting a conspiracy. Does that mean they're in CAHOOTS?

I just bought a scary sound effects record. It can be played in "MOAN-otone or SCARY-o!"

IKEA is at it again. Unlike their meatballs, there's no "HORSING Around!"
They're financing a remake of an H.G Wells story. It's called "The FUD of the Gods!"

If sea captains christen ships with bottles of champagne, do winos christen toilets with bottles of Viper?

A *Clockwork Orange* is a Stanley Kubrick film. A "KlokWirk Ornj" is a colorful timepiece at IKEA.

Def Jam Records wants to remake *Three on a Meathook* and call it, "Three on a Phat Beat Hook!"

What do you call the ventriloquist dummy from *Magic* when drenched in water?
"Saturated FATS!"

Hear about the French ghost?
He's good for a "MOAN Sheri" or two.

What kind of candy does the Crawling
Eye give out, for Halloween?
"Candy CORNEAS!"

What would you call Esther Forbes' novel
if it was horror themed?
"Johnny TreMANIAC!"

I heard punk rock aliens just landed
their UFO! They're stomping around in
their Doc MARTIANS!

What does a ghost wear on a boat?
An "AFTERLIFE Vest!"

Guillotine operators don't like the band
Men Without Hats. They prefer Men
Without Heads!

Skeletons just want the "barebones
facts."

Hear about the city living vampire?

He enjoys the hustle and bustle of blood
corpuscles!

What Biz Markie lyric was influenced by Wes Craven?
"You say he's a DEADLY Friend! You say say he's a DEADLY Friend!"

What Prince song is about the Incredible Shrinking Man's car?
"LITTLE Red Corvette!"

Which Rush song do Mediums and Psychics like?
"SPIRIT of Radio!"

What city makes Quasimodo's heart race?
"BELL-Fast!"

Stephen King's Pennywise was originally a cartoonist. He'd ask, "Want a THOUGHT balloon?"

Did you know the Deadly Mantis got a tattoo?
It says "BUG 4 LIFE!"

Hear about the Beatles song influenced by a zombie lady?

It's called, "Ela-GNAW Rigormotis!"

Warlock Time Line
1965 Paul Lynde was Warlock Uncle Arthur on *Bewitched*.
1966 Superman fights a warlock in a cartoon.
1989 Julian Sands stars in *Warlock.*
2011 Charlie Sheen proclaims to be a warlock.
Where did the magic go?

What Moon Unit Zappa song is about dinosaurs and cowboys?
"Valley of the Gwangi Girl!"
It's prehistorical, to the max!

When ghosts use dry measure, they put four pecks in a "BOO-shel."

If only Dorian Gray had Photoshop...

"The Descent" is a horror film.
The D-scent is an aroma from Kathy Griffin's "D List!"

What film stars Charlton Heston as a "Mamma Monster" fan?
"The Ome-GAGA Man!"

What film finds Charlton Heston getting attacked by British punk rockers?
The "OI- mega Man!"

The Brain That Wouldn't Die was a talking head that claimed to have power. Mmmmmmm... sounds like Bill O'Reily!

Why did the hangman go to the plastic surgeon?
For a "NOOSE job!"

What do you get by crossing a cryptozoology legend and unleavened bread?
The "MOTHzaman!"

What Stephen King story is about vampiric online bidders?
"Salem's Ebay Lot!"

What film has Bela Lugosi as upper management?

The Human Resources Monster!

What film has a Great Lakes bride
having a devil of a time?
Highway Hell Michigan!

How do you tell Godzilla a joke?
You say, "STOMP me if you've heard this
one."

What Canadian city makes vampire
coffins?
"CASKEToon!"

What *American Werewolf in London*
influenced act sings O.P.P.?
"David Naughton by Nature!"

What film stars Ice Cube and the
Abominable Snow Man?
"Are We There, YETI?"

What William Shatner film is about
fighting off sunbathing senior citizens?
"Kingdom of the Spider Veins!"

I watched the werewolf film *Silver Bullet*. It's really high "CALIBER."

In *The Screaming Skull*, a woman loses her mind while living in her husband's dead wife's home.
In "The Streaming Skull," a woman gets to use her husband's dead wife's Netflix account, and loses the password!

The Crawling Eye has been showing signs of an improved mood. It's safe to say he's been on an "OPTIC."

In what Robert Deniro film does his character blather, babble, and talk gibberish?
"Taxi DRIVEL!"

Who has the better Wrecking Ball, Miley Cyrus or The Tall Man?

What style do you get by crossing HR Giger's work with a Louisiana swamp?
"BAYOU-mechanics!"

What do you get by crossing a film with Giger poster art and a James Bond film? "A VIEW to a Future Kill!"

Every now and then, Strange Jason throws me a theme for the show and I have to actually use my brain!

Here are a few to spotlight:
Horror and Wrestling mashups
Fifties TV and horror mashups
Cartoons and horror mashups.

So, in this ring, we have wrestling and horror!!

Hear about the "Iron SHRIEK?"

Aha! Can you smell what the Monstermatt is cooking?!

What do you get by crossing a Peter Straub novel and a wrestler with a giant exotic bird?
"KOKO B. Ware!"

What wrestler comes straight from Hell?

"John CENAbite!"

What kind of wrestling match features the Manster and Duane & Belial Bradley from Basket Case?
A Tag Team match!

I hear they're trying to bring SANTO to social media by making him a "Figure FourSquare Leglock app!"

Did you know they used to call me "The Fabulous Mwhoouhuhahala?"

The Toxic Avenger borrows a move from Chief Jay Strongbow, with the "TROMAhawk Chop!"

What fictitious company tried to sponsor Jim "The ANVIL" Neinhardt?
ACME!

What wrestling manager do zombies love?
Bobby "The BRAIN" Heenan!

Don't change that channel...

We have some Atomic Age TV...

We found "Father Knows BEAST!"

What's Dracula's favorite TV show?
"BAT Masterson!"

What old game show do zombies and ghouls like?
"BRAINS & BRAWN!"

What game show is for scifi buffs?
"The Crawling Eyes Have It!"

There's a show tailor-made for horror fans. It's called,
"Four SCAR Playhouse!"

What old TV show follows a ghoulish Norwegian family?
"I Dismember Mamma!"

What TV show has cowboys and a Japanese videotape?
Johnny "RINGU!"

What show is loved by coroners?
"My Little MORGUE-y!"

What old show does the Incredible
Shrinking Man like?
"Small Fry Club!"

What show usually played two episodes
or a "double header?"
"Follow That Manster!"

Then, it's off to the comic strips...
With the success of "Afterlife With
Archie" we want...

"Bringing up Father From His Grave."
Maggie has to deal with Jiggs in this
afterlife adventure!

"Dondi of the Dead"
A comic about a zombified orphan.

"Gorefield" a cat who kills (literally) for
lasagna.

"Beetle Boil-ley"

A soldier gets nominated for the "Nobel PUS Prize!"

"For Better or Curse!"
A Canadian family of voodoo priests and priestesses.

"Rex MORGUE-an M.D."
A doctor with ghoulish intentions... is met with a few cold shoulders.

"Andy DeCaPPitated"
A bloke loses a round of darts, then loses his head!

Okay, okay. Those are horrible!

Oh, look! I just got an invite from the Two Thousand Maniacs. It's to a Southern party. It says RSVP only with "reGRITS."

What song by the Cramps involves nudity and an M.C. Escher painting? "Naked Girl Falling up the Stairs!"

Hannibal Lecter is a Cramps fan. One of his favorite songs to serenade his victims is "You Got Good Taste." The other song is "Eyeball in my Martini."

Contrary to Igor's beliefs, I do not hail from "Dope Island." The Cramps know of some fiends there.

Maniacs, I'll close this chapter of hilarity (yeah, right) with two jokes about Sir Christopher Lee, who passed away this year. Lee portrayed my favorite version of Dracula. A tribute? In a way.

What Scifi show had Christopher Lee as a big spending "Foodie?"
SPICE $19.99

And finally, this one is my 1700th Bad Monster Joke. Yes, you read it right. I feel lucky to have celebrated some of the greats every hundredth- and the one-thousandth joke. It's fitting and timely that this one is Christopher Lee...

What film stars Christopher Lee as a chocolate-loving vampire?
"Dracula has RIESEN from the Grave!"

WHAT UNDERGROUND STOOGES
SLAPPED EACH OTHER AROUND THE
TIME MACHINE?

THE MOELOCKS!

Troma Jokes

What do you get by crossing a Carvel ice cream cake and Kabukiman?
"Sgt. Kabukipuss!"

What Troma Classic targets toxic e-readers?
"The Class of NOOK 'em High!"

What do you get by crossing the Feudal system and a Troma film?
"SERF Nazis Must Die!"

What do you get by crossing Troma, tennis and Bigfoot?
"Yeti: A LOVE Story!"

What do you get by crossing Troma and a device that lamely turns lights "on and off?"
"Tales from the CLAPPER!"

What Troma film finds Toxie trying to stave off a case of scurvy?
"CITRUS in Toxie!"

What do you get by crossing a love story, Troma and Miracle Whip?
"Tro-MAYO and Juliet!"

What do you get by crossing FOWL rhymes and Troma?
"Poetry-Geist!"

Which group of bodybuilding mutants terrorized Nuke 'Em High?
The "CREATINS!"

What film has a clash between commandos and dermatologists?
"Troma's WART!"

What film is about a veteran on a spiritual journey?

"Combat CHAKRA!"

What River flows next to Nuke 'Em High?
The "PoTROMAc!"

A FEW THINGS ON MY MIND...

Lunch Meat Jokes

What film is about killer rednecks
throwing burgers?
"LAUNCH Meat!"

Hear about the redneck killers that serve
a late morning meal?
Their tale is "BRUNCH Meat!"

What film has Australian redneck killers
turning people into burgers?
"Lunch MATE!"

What film has killer rednecks forgetting
to debone their victims?
"CRUNCH Meat!"

The *Lunch Meat* crew would gather for a
"Night Cap-icola!"

What film has burgers made from crumpled people?
"SCRUNCH Meat!"

What do you get by crossing *Lunch Meat* and the artist of *The Scream*?
"MUNCH Meat!"

What film has intuitive killer rednecks?
"HUNCH Meat!"

What film has redneck killers making burgers out of plumbers?
"PLUNGE Meat!"

Did you know *Lunch Meat* had two directors?
Their names were "Oscar & Meyer!"

What film turns professional boxers into burgers?
"Punch Meat!"

Who was the producer of *Lunch Meat*?
"Mort-Adella!"

And that's no baloney!

I gave some tools to a Golem.
He informed me that somebody stole 'em.
It's a no-brainer, they took the wood
planer, which was meant for the Golem's
chafing Solum.

The Stand Jokes

The TV series *The Stand* gave us "Captain Trips." Who was the original? Dick Van Dyke!

What is Tom Cullen's favorite book? "Goodnight, M-O-O-N!" Laws, yes.

What Tom Cullen phrase can be used when you buy two Jude Law films and a Yes CD?
"LAWS, YES!"

What do you get by crossing a Stephen King miniseries about Randal Flagg and a Monty Python bit about a dead parrot?
"The STUNNED!"

Who has the better "Captain Tripps", *The Stand* or Priceline?

The people from both Mother Abigail and Randal Flagg's camps would rather band together for a free WIFI zone!

Which character is like a strong Swedish wind?
Mother "ABBA GALE!"

After *The Stand*, Trashcan Man was hoping to audition for *Stomp* and put those cans to good use!

Which one of Frank Zappa's kids is Tom Cullen's favorite?
M-O-O-N Unit Zappa!

What's the Trashcan Man's favorite part of tennis?
"MATCH Point!"

What is the Trashcan Man's favorite 80's film?
"Weekend at BURN-ies!"

What TV game show does the Trashcan Man love?
"MATCH Game!"

WHO WAS THE PERPLEXED GOD THAT
BOONE MET IN MIDIAN?

"BAFFLE-MET!"

Nightbreed Jokes

What do you get by crossing a daydreamer with Clive Barker's underground city of monsters?
"The Secret Life of Walter MIDIAN!"

Hear about the Midian phone company? They have a great long distance "CABAL-ing" plan!

Who was the perplexed God that Boone met in Midian?
"BAFFLE-met!"

Which Midian God was made of a mass of bubbles?
"BaFOAMet!"

What group of monsters loved flying things in the air?

"KITEbreed!"

What is Peloquin's favorite Air Supply song?
"Every Human in the World is MEAT!"

What TV show combines Archie Bunker and *Nightbreed*?
"CABAL in the Family!"

Which one of Boone's psychiatrists used to own a tour bus?
Dr. Double Decker!

What Nightbreed city stood for an indefinite amount of time?
"Mid-EON!"

How do you know Peloquin was influenced by Brad Pitt?
He told Boone, "Don't talk about Nightbreed Club!"

What do you get by crossing an 80's sitcom with a Clive Barker film?
"Nightbreed Court!"

Where do the Midian monsters shop?
"Bed, Baphomet and Beyond!"

QUASIMODO WENT TO THE NYSE.
HE JUST WANTED TO RING THE OPENING BELL!

Rancid Rhymes/Sordid Songs

A dillar, a dollar. How do you make the Wolfman holler? You carefully hide all of his FLEA COLLARS!

A dollar, a dollar. Try driving Dracula insane, by putting "road closed" signs along your neck veins.

Ligeia. Dear Ligeia. You sit inside your tomb. Come join me in some classic video gaming and we'll play a few rounds of KABOOM!

Creature. Dear Creature. While you chase minnows in your lagoon, be mindful of bigger fish who'll chase you as they wish.

I just watched *The Keep* and I say it without jest. Although it held a creature, it couldn't hold my interest. I had the film ready with a feeling of hope. But, halfway through it, I just couldn't cope.

I think my monster-in-law has had too many formaldehyde toddies. She's pickled! Her face is contorted and she looks like Don Rickles!

Mummy. Oh, Mummy. With your bandages taut. When you're angry, is the gauze bound in a knot?

Ring of ghouls around a cadaver.
Save the skin for after.
Nip at the toes. Sauté the nose.
Don't drop the eyeballs or they'll scatter!

The Fool on the Bill
(Tune of "Fool on the Hill")

Take after take,
Quiet on the set.

This won't be understated at all; that's a sure bet!
No can look away, the screeners is getting chewed.
So get your popcorn out, because here comes...

The Fool on the Bill,
Like Jim Carey or Jack Black,
Act so over the top,
They just can't dial it back!

(Tune of "Maria")

How do you dissolve a problem like Maria?
How does one prepare an "acid bath?"
"Breaking Bad" showed a way,
"Scream and Scream Again" did so too, in its day.
Oh, how do you dissolve a problem like Maria?
It's not an open ended question, to provoke some indigestion,
at the slightest suggestion,

To get rid of some upstart... In... Your...
Path!

"What I Did For Love"

Kiss your grave goodbye.
You know you must be going.
You're back from the dead, and it
appears,
That you're a roaming schmuck,
Rundown by a truck; now you're a
ghost.

Learn how to haunt,
The world is yours to conquer,
So , don't idle-ly sit.
Get on the move, you can't haunt
certain towns, without permits!

Boooooo!
It's so overused.
Try another line,
Haunt so you'll be remembered.

For what you did to scare...
For what you did to scare...

———

(Tune of "Does Anybody Know What Time it is?")

As I was walking down Elm Street one day.
A man came up to me, with the worst sweater that I've seen and asked if I had any bad dreams, yeah.
And I said...

I don't dream so much anymore,
(What happened to Ya?)
I got a real bad case of sleep apnea,

(No)
I got no time for you and your goofy glove and hat,
I'd sleep anywhere, but my apnea gear won't lay flat.

Tinker, Tailor, Soldier, Spy.
Stick a needle in my eye.
If I don't die, but "wake and bake,"

Rush me to 7 Eleven for nachos and
Frosted Flakes!

A Zombie came into my den,
I asked it to walk, not traipse.
I feared it might run its rot on the good
set of drapes.

The Wolfman looked at his reflection
with despair.
He noticed he had a new batch of gray
hairs.
He called his hairstylist to get rid of the
grays,
But she can't schedule him until the next
moon phase.

A monster from Duluth, ran a kissing
booth.
Eating onions all day, keeping smooches
away.
Halitosis, the diagnosis, for this stinky
truth.

A ghoul went to city hall, wanting a permit to open coffins. The mayor declined it, heavily fined it, then said, "You'd be better off opening doors at any Baskin & Robbins!"

Manster. Oh, MANSTER. Go paint the town red. I'm sure you'll do it twice as fast than most, because of your two heads.

A zombie shambled to the window, to look at the sky and its vast expanse. He was embarrassed to realize that he wasn't wearing pants!

A ghoul looked for love in all the wrong places. Attics, cellars and a few crawl spaces. If only he got the gist; he could find a hook up on Tinder or Craigslist.

Ashes to ashes, something to whatever. I don't think this will be very clever. I had hope, but it went. Like vapors blown out an air vent!

An energy surge has blown out the crypt's electrical fuses. I "axed" old Frankenstein to share his electrode juice, but he simply refuses.

Honey BooBoo go blow the horn, in your momma 'a redneck dream ride; an F150 Ford.

My fear, my dearie, is not the music of Conway Twitty. But rather, the thought of another sequel to "Sex and the City."

I have an urge for a funeral dirge. It's much better than a waltz. But, my partner is lost and at a large cost. Because I'm thirsty and she has our chocolate malts.

Video stores give us horrors. Ghastly, bloody and ghoulish. I too, was a video store clerk, didn't act like a jerk. Even when the customers were being quite foolish. I would say," thank you for your business "and "I'll see you sooner than 'late-ah'."

When asked what I meant, I explained,"You rented a VHS player with tapes that are clearly BETA!"

It's raining, it's pouring. The old vampire bat is soaring. Across the lake, to flee the stakes, that Van Helsing is "carving and scoring."

Frankenstein. Dear Monster Frankenstein.
Unjam your finger from your nose, you dolt!
Why not jam it into a wall outlet and get a hundred or so tasty volts!

Dr. Jekyll and Mr. Hyde.
One of you has to start winning at the track and "get off the Schneid."

Ghouls drool at the sight of fresh coffins. Tasting the fruit within and do some noshing. It makes their tastebuds do some moshing.

Godzilla. Dear Godzilla.
You overgrown radioactive thing.

Why not wrap some shiny railroad tracks a round your neck and give yourself some "bling!"

RODAN. Dear RODAN.
Please tell us one thing.
Do you drink tons of RedBull?
Because, you definitely have some wings!

Wolfman. Dear Wolfman.
Our last round of "Your Mamma" jokes got quite a few chuckles. But, you've gotta admit only one of our Mammas has such furry knuckles!

Dracula. Dear Dracula.
Don't look at my neck, take heed. I'm pretty sure Alice Cooper stated that "Only Women Bleed."

Manitou. Dear Manitou.
I hear you up to your old tricks. Just like Dennis Deyoung and his band perform the music, but they can't call themselves STYX.

Pennywise. Hey you clown, Pennywise! I don't think it's nice to gloat. Because, you bought your balloons with leftover interest from a mortgage rate that floats!

A zombie was rotting. Things were falling off. His decayed unmentionables hit the floor, when his doctor told him to "turn and cough!"

I dropped it like it's hot, for fear I'd burn my fingers.
Fear spawns a creature inside us, just like William Castle's "Tingler."

WHAT BIZ MARKIE LYRIC WAS INFLUENCED BY WES CRAVEN?

"YOU, GOT WHAT I NEED. YOU SAY 'HE'S A DEADLY FRIEND. YOU SAY HE'S A DEADLY FRIEND!"

CHUCKY AND THE KID

Rancid Rhymes/Sordid Songs part 2

Hey, Hey! We're the Zombies! People say we shamble around. We're too busy escaping our graves, we won't stay put in the ground!

Howling at the moon, the werewolf made it known, that he'd eat old Mother Hubbard if her cupboards held no bones.

In 1965 Frankenstein tried conquering the world. He couldn't follow through. He fought Baragon and fell under the earth. Sadly, there's not much you can do.

A slice, a hack. Put it in a sack. Fear not, for it's loaves of bread, not bodies my blade does face. Here's an end piece; care to have a taste?

For this giant with one eye, it is hard to observe, any line, angle or curve. This is why the Amazing Colossal Man has got some nerve. Thinking he can drive with his remaining closed eye, and not once even swerve.

Issac Newton was disputin' about things going up and coming down. He stumbled upon a theory that future generations might think profound. If a reality show celebrity falls in the forest, does it make a sound?

A voodoo priestess laid things on the table. They were from ports unknown. Eyeballs, blood, a foot. Even a heart that was kaput! A bucket of animal bones. Why did she do it? To get better Dish Network reception in her home.

During a schoolyard argument, I said to I'm Ho Tep, "Don't accuse me of taking your "Lunch Mummy!" Don't get your gauze in a bunch. I can loan you the dough for lunch."

I gave him enough for the meal and a pretzel. He asked if I wanted the change. I told him to leave the change for Dr. Jekyll.

I gave some tools to a Golem. He informed me that somebody stole 'em. It's a no-brainer, they took the wood planer, which was meant for the Golem's chafing Solum.

I don't want her, you can have her. I could shove her under a ladder, with a black cat, stepping on cracks and breaking mirrors. Triskaidekaphobia, ain't one of my fears.

If Jason Voorhees knew you were coming, he would have baked a cake. But, then he'd lop off your head and put it on a stake! As soon as you arrived at Camp Crystal Lake- How'd Ya do, How'd Ya do, How'd Ya do!

The Toxic Avenger had a mop. With it, he'd fight crime. When he had some down time, he'd take that mop and clean up the grime. A janitor by trade, with toxic waste: this hideously deformed creature of super human size and strength was made.

The film *Transcendence* has a dependence, on your ability to suspend disbelief. Johnny Depp's living in a computer, still making women swoon. How? Is his computer loaded with free songs from ITunes?

You say Geeger, I say Giger.
I say Giger and you say Geeger.
Geeger, Giger. Giger, Geeger.
Let's call the whole thing off!

1 tequila, 2 tequilas, 3 tequilas, floor. Puking out an H. R. Giger worm in *Poltergeist 2* is a nice taste of horror.

Machete doesn't tweet. Machete doesn't text. He does wander around scowling. Why? Did someone force him to watch the sequels of *The Howling*?

Don't go to Camp Crystal Lake, it'll be a big mistake. Especially, if you want to live. Jason will be sure come after you, with a machete, axe or shiv.

Mudder. Fadder. Please send me cake. The food is bad here, at Camp Crystal Lake. And one more thing, I have to ask- who's the lurking creep in the hockey mask?!

The bats will leave the belfry,
With their wings a flip-flapping.
If the vampire doesn't get blood soon, it's her lips that will be chapping.

Duane Bradley from "Basket Case" sings...
"I'm putting my brother Belial, in a wicker basket..."

Vampira sings...

"I've got a large amount, saved in my blood bank account."

What could be scarier than R.L. Stein's *Goosebumps*? Any hint of another Eddie Murphy film starring the KLUMPS!

(Tune of "Jingle Bells")

Jingle bats,
Big black cats,
Shrieking all the way!
Haunted homes and catacombs,
Embalmings twice a day...

(Tune of "I'll Be Home for Christmas")

I'll be embalming for Christmas,
You can autopsy me.
Have some gauze,
Crank up the saws,
There's rigor mortis in my knee.

I feel like I'm accident prone. It's definitely a curse.

The Tall Man ran over me for the third time today, with his hearse!

(Tune of *The William Tell Overture*)

When the strangest things do occur, they call on Roger Whitaker. Solving things like mysteries, he does it all for a small fee.

His whistling attracts tons of ghosts, he snags them all from coast to coast. He's not here to lay down a rap; he lulls them into a big trap!

(Tune of "Heartbreak Hotel")

Well, since my baby left me.
I found a new place to dwell. There's Norman's taxidermy animals, in the Bates Hotel.

Don't know if I should shower there, baby. Don't know if I should shower. Because if I shower there, I could die!

A sniffle, a snuffle.
What the heck is a "Kerfuffle?"
I like zombies in a mid-tempo shuffle.
They will attack. Your skull for a snack.
Eating your brains like truffles.

Should he continue, moshing on the
victim's sinew? This is the immediate
question. Every so often... even zombies
get indigestion.

"Ermmmmehgerd!"

There's something in the lab. Lying on
the slab. A fiend, with furiously flying
digits. It's texting with emojis.
My needlework isn't holding. While
leaning on a shelf, she tried taking a
selfie. Popped the stitches and lost some
toesies.

The toes I ate were blood red.
The eyes you ate were blue.
Dearest Zelda the Zombie.
If you weren't undead, I'd eat you too.

Blacula Road (tune of "Tobacco Road")

I sleep in, a sort of trunk.
Don't like the daylight, I think it's bunk.
I came from Africa, where I was a
prince.
Is there anywhere in L.A. to get a
blintz?!

Flying around to discotheques.
Looking for babes with great necks.
I found Tina, the "love of my life."
Just so happens she's my reincarnated
wife!

But I roam. My thirst keeps me on the
go!
You know it drives me batty...
Blacula Road!

(Tune of "Grand Old Flag")

He's Randall Flag,
The Walking Man Flag,

And he's a beast, walking behind the
rows.
He likes to swim, this "Walter O'Dim",
In people's dreads and woes.

In the works of King,
He keeps appearing,
Where in the heck will it go?
If he comes to you in denim and flowing
hair,
Call Mother Abagail and get the heck out
of there!

(Tune of "Swanee")

Karloff! How we love Ya!
How we love Ya!
Dear Boris Karloff!

You've played characters, of every kind.
But, of course our all-time favorite is
that monster that they call Frankenstein!

(Tune of "Spell on You")

I put a Spellcheck on you. Because, you're MIME.
Stop the THEMES that you DEW.
I ain't LIME.

(Tune of "16 Tons")

You write sixteen words and what do you get.
It ain't a Haiku, but add one more and I'll bet.
It will meet the structure and I ain't lyin',
Fit them in three lines and you're doin' just fine...

HEAR ABOUT THE CADAVER COMEDIAN?

HIS TAG LINE IS "WELL EXHUUUMME , ME!"

The Afterword

Dear Reader,

    I can't believe you made it to the end of this "book." You either must be a masochist or you've just taken the world's largest bowel movement, and either way you've certainly earned my respect. I first had the displeasure of meeting "Monster" Matt Patterson in 2012 when I was producing *Return to Nuke 'Em High: Volumes 1 & 2* for Troma Entertainment.

    After being subjected to a few of what he claimed were jokes, I was convinced he had shown up on set to gather new material for his next terrible book. As the production went on, he began to show me drafts of his new tome. I was appalled.

Patterson was obviously inspired by his surroundings, but even I was taken back at how he far surpassed the lewdness and crudeness of Troma's brand of sex and slime. I was even more shocked when he told me he was going to publish the material under his new pen name, which he had scrawled repeatedly in our men's room, Master Shatt Splatterson.

I advised the now drooling Mr. Patterson that while his new work was ambitious, his fans might not comprehend, much less stomach, the change in direction. Luckily, he took my advice, and after recovering from the Troma experience, penned this much more politically correct, but equally atrocious, effort.

Justin Martell
Producer, *Return to Nuke 'Em High: Volume 1 & 2* and other films which no one has seen.
P.S. Zac Amico assisted in writing this afterward because I, like Mr. Patterson, am not funny.

About the Author
Monstermatt Patterson

Monstermatt Patterson, The Man of a Thousand Bad Monster Jokes, is a monster of many talents. He started this journey into horror and monsters in the winter of 2006 following shoulder surgery.

His work (Writing or Illustration) are featured in:

Rack Toys: Cheap, Crazed Playthings

Steampunk Originals Vol.2

Death Shriek Comics

We Love Monsters Magazine

He regularly appears on the Rondo-nominated 6 Foot Plus horror podcast. He also appears on Tomb TV and other podcasts and shows.

Films:
(acting, fx, producing, art dept, etc.)

Sledge, Return to Nuke 'Em High Vol.1&2, The American Side, Dry Bones, A Grim Becoming, Dick Johnson and Tommygun vs. The Cannibal Cop, Born To Die, Fable: Teeth of Beasts, Gore, The Nught and Final Day, To Release a Soul,

Summer Camp Party, Superheroes Don't Need Capes

Honors:

Nominee-2009 Best Sculptor, Artvoice Best of Buffalo Awards

Emcee- 2010 Buffalo Monster Fest

Nominee-2013 Best Painter, Artvoice Best of Buffalo Awards

Nominee- 2011, 2012, 2013, 2014

6FtPlus- Best Podcast, Rondo Hatton Horror Awards

Winner-2014 Best Painter

Artvoice Best of Buffalo Awards

Winner-2014 (Ha-Ha! Horror, Best in Humor Books) President's Choice Gold Medal - Florida Authors and Publishers Association Awards.